MW01259080

Signed Books and more
www.mattshawpublications.co.uk

THE

MARIANA

TRENCH

Matt Shaw

In Loving Memory of Billy Smith.

A giant among men.

A true friend.

One hell of a reader.

Chapter One

BEFORE

During the daylight hours, the sea looked inviting with its turquoise waters gently lapping at the beach's golden sands of what was once - before the tsunami - considered one of the finest resorts in the country, if not the world. Despite the destruction all around - felled palm trees, seaweed scattered far and wide, debris from the half-demolished buildings, along with whatever was dragged up from the depths of the ocean and spat out - you could almost still *hear* what the beach would have been like before the disaster, if you really concentrated. People would have been frolicking in the waters, laughing, screaming whilst being splashed by their friends, quiet music coming from the poolside bar up on the resort itself, gulls crying overhead as they watch out for dropped food to scavenge. Now though there was an eerie silence broken only by the susurration of the sea which, with night having already fallen, looked far more sinister with waters now black and seemingly bottomless within just a few feet of the shoreline.

John Drain was standing on the beach troubled by mixed emotions. On the one hand, it was hard to ignore those who had perished here. Those poor sons of bitches had saved for months, some maybe even years, to come to this "little slice of paradise" and yet the pounds and dollars they'd paid weren't quite enough as they then went on to pay further, with their lives. It hadn't just been the resort that took the full brunt of the tsunami either. The giant wave had flattened everything much further inland too, taking yet more lives in what had been reported as one of the greatest catastrophes ever recorded. On the other hand though, John couldn't help but feel a buzz of excitement because of the reason he had come out here in the first place. He had spent years, and a vast proportion of his obscene wealth, to get out here and into the waters to see the Mariana Trench for himself and, finally, he was going to do just that but there was an even greater reason to be excited. What had once meant as a trip for him, and any others willing to pay a substantial fee, had become an important field trip in which scientists could get down to the trench and investigate what was happening down there. Initially his trip was going to get in a few magazines, no doubt, with journalists taking aim at him for how he wanted to spend his money. No doubt they would call him "crazy" for wanting to see what was down there for himself and some would criticise him for wasting his money when, really, it could have gone into charities but - whatever. It was his money and he often wondered whether they would donate their fortune, should they suddenly find themselves with heavy pockets. They talked the talk in their magazines, papers and online blogs whenever they spoke of him (or any rich person) but if the shoe were on the other foot and he was the one doing the reporting, John wondered what *their* story would be. Besides which, he made generous charity payments and would continue to do so. He just didn't advertise the fact because he found it crass to do so. He paid into the charities to help, not so he could get recognition. Anyway, the trip was more than his "little sight-seeing" project now that the scientists were going with him. It would still feature in magazines and such but now, given they were going down to investigate the trench and strange activity down there, it would also feature in science books where their findings would be reported. Yes, he probably wouldn't have much to report back on but it was his money and his specially-made submarine which would allow them to go down and spend a month undersea watching and monitoring everything. That alone was surely worth a name check in the science books.

John smiled to himself. He'd always been hopeless at science, back in his school days all those years ago, and yet now look at him. He thought, *Mr. Cross would be proud.*

'Beautiful isn't it?' Becca Ross said as she approached him. John visibly jumped at the sound of her voice. He'd been so lost in deep thought, he hadn't heard her approaching. As far as he was aware, he was the only one on the resort with most of the workers, trying to get the place fixed up, having already left for the night. Becca laughed. 'Sorry, I didn't meant to startle you.' She extended her hand and introduced herself, 'Becca Ross. I'm one of the…'

John took her hand in his and shook. 'I know who you are,' he said with a smile. 'I studied all the files ahead of coming out. I'm…'

'John Drain,' Becca said. 'And I studied all of the files too.' She asked, 'Are we the only ones here?'

'Other than the crew, so far.'

Becca stood next to John and looked out into the ocean. 'It really is beautiful, isn't it?'

John just smiled. He could see why some would find the ocean beautiful but, to him, it was just haunting at night, mainly thanks to his imagination and the fear that, really, there could be anything lurking within those waters, unseen and waiting to strike. There was also the thought of how many people had lost their lives in the sea; not just this stretch of water but all around the world. As John looked out into the vast blackness, he couldn't help but to wonder how many lost souls were out there, in the darkness unable to find their way back? The longer he stood there, the longer he was sure he could hear their cries with each lapping of the waves against the shore. A shiver ran the length of his spine and he turned his back to the ocean, unable to look at it any longer. As he started to walk away, Becca quickly followed.

'I just wanted to say thank you for this,' she said.

'Not a problem. I'm glad you came.'

'Are you kidding? I feel like Dr. Alan Grant when he was invited to go and visit *Jurassic Park*.'

'Does that make me John Hammond?'

'You do share the same name.'

'Hopefully this expedition will go slightly better than Jurassic Park.'

'Well there's less velociraptors for one, so that's a good start.' Becca laughed at the thought of dinosaurs running around down there.

'I'm surprised you made a Jurassic Park reference,' John said as he thought back to what she originally said.

'Well I mean I was going to make a *Deep Blue Sea* reference but I couldn't remember the names of the characters in it and not as many people have seen that film so… Jurassic Park it was!'

John laughed. 'I've seen it. Hopefully this little trip won't go the same way as that film either.'

'You don't happen to know if any of the crew are coming onboard with a parrot, do you?' Becca was making reference to LL Cool J's "chef" character in the film *Deep Blue Sea* who, for reasons known only to the writers, had brought an irritating parrot with him.

John just smiled. 'Come, I'll introduce you to the crew.'

*

NOW

The captain of the submarine, Commander Chris Combs, had gone deathly pale as he turned to those who'd gathered.

The faces of both crew and scientists looked at him with hope in their eyes. Solemnly he shook his head.

'Whatever it is, it has got us and it isn't in a hurry to let go. At this moment in time, we're trapped and unless it decides to just release us there's only two ways this is going to go.' They waited for him to explain further. He continued, 'One; it crushes the submarine. I don't need to explain what happens then. Two; it just holds us here until the oxygen supplies run out.' He stopped talking. A few people - already on the verge of tears - broke down and openly wept. Others just stood there with a shocked expression on their faces as they processed everything they'd heard, and all that had happened.

John turned away from the group and walked to the viewing window; an eighteen inch thick screen which allowed people to look out to the mysterious world beyond. This trip was supposed to be a once in a lifetime experience, the chance to see things that no other living person had seen before. An expedition into the unknown and, due to the nature of the voyage, no weapon systems had been built into the submarine he designed. In hindsight… John let out a quiet sigh. That oversight looked like it was going to cost everyone on board their lives and whilst he could not have predicted any of this, he was still responsible. He wanted to apologise to each and every person but he knew the words he'd say would mean nothing. At the end of the day, they'd all still die and it would still be his fault.

Victoria Hill, the medical officer, entered the room with an unsettling quickness in her pace. Commander Chris Combs knew from the way she moved there was a problem without her needing to say anything.

'What is it?' he asked, almost fearful for the answer.

'It's Becca,' Victoria said. 'You need to come and see this.'

Chapter Two

BEFORE

A tender had been laid on to transport those going on the expedition across to where the submarine - their home for the next month - floated in the deeper water. Before the tsunami there'd been options where the sub could dock and they could have boarded but, now, most of those docks had been entirely destroyed without a trace of them remaining. The Mariana Islands were just a ruin; a shadow of the paradise isles they once had been.

'And there she is,' John said with the same excitement as a new father showing off his baby. 'I won't tell you the costs involved in creating her, but there she most definitely is...'

The submarine he had created, Deep-sea Challenger IV, didn't look much different to a normal submarine but the workings were entirely more advanced. So much so, in fact, that the U.S army had approached John with a contract for him to build another just as soon as he was finished with his expedition. Although, not a fan of warfare, the contract was currently sitting on his office desk, back in New Zealand.

'The fourth Deep-sea Challenger? If I'm not mistaken there was only one before this which was used for the film director James Cameron's expedition?' Nate Stephenson said. Nate, one of the world's leading seismologists, had come along to witness the many quakes taking place undersea with his own eyes. He wasn't an expert on the Mariana Trench but had looked at a few websites before heading out and the one he spent the most amount of time on, happened to be the one which spoke about the Deep-sea Challenger's expedition.

John smiled at him. 'That's right. You've done your research, I see. Good for you.'

'Well surely that makes this the Deep-sea Challenger II?'

John laughed. 'Unfortunately not.' He downed the last of his Coke, straight from the can, and then held the can out towards Nate. With a squeeze of his hand, he crushed it flat. The can crumpled with ease and, once done, John opened his hand again to show off the can. 'That's what happened to numbers II and III.' He added, 'There's a lot of pressure down there…'

Nate's face dropped. He looked towards the submarine as it seamlessly floated on the water's surface. 'You thoroughly tested this one, right?'

'Well we went to about half the depth we're actually going to and it creaked a few times but, yeah, it seemed to hold up just fine so we're pretty confident,' John said. Of course he was just teasing; the submarine had been tested, tested, tested and tested again before they'd got to this stage - and not just to the pressure they were going to experience at the bottom of the ocean but almost double that too.

Seeing Nate's concerned look, marine biologist Becca leaned closer to him and whispered, 'I'm guessing you didn't read the reports about the Deep-Sea Challenger IV?' She shook her head, playfully disappointed with Nate. 'It was impressive stuff.' She added, 'You don't want to know how many years it took to develop and the costs involved. All I'll say is, you probably don't want to accidentally break anything in there.' Her words brought little comfort to Nate who was still imagining what it would be like to be inside a crushed can.

The tender pulled up to the side of the submarine, close to where the hatch was which would take those boarding down into the depths of the impressive submarine.

Commander Chris Combs, whom some had met the previous night before he and the rest of the crew came over, was there to greet them and help them onboard. Despite most of the scientists being highly trained, and skilled, in their fields of expertise - this was the first time most of them had even seen a submarine, let alone boarded one.

Today was all about getting settled onboard the sub. Everyone would find their cabins, they would be shown around the submarine and given as many of the safety procedures as they needed to know at that particular moment. They would then be given the night to get comfortable and be sure they were happy with being so confined and - by morning - when everything was ready, they would begin the dive. Most were keen just to get going so as to see what the Trench offered but, a few were grateful for that last minute opportunity to pull out, if they weren't happy to continue further given, apart from in the case of an emergency, there would be no return to the surface until after the thirty days they'd been paid upfront for.

*

NOW

Becca tossed and turned on her bunk bed. Her once brown eyes had turned almost black, the same colour as the deep-waters. Her hair was matted together in damp knots and her skin was clammy to the touch with little beads of sweat here and there. She cried out in pain as she crawled her nails down the side of cabin.

Victoria came back in. She'd brought Chris down with her, along with John. Both men stopped in the cabin's doorway when they saw the state of Becca. They'd both known she had been unwell, ever since being exposed to *it* but this was the worst they'd seen her.

Victoria turned to them gravely and said, 'And I've given her the maximum dose of morphine I can give and…' Becca was still screaming in pain despite the drugs. 'But then there is this…' Victoria sat on the edge of the bunk bed and raised Becca's top to expose her belly. Both the men stepped back in shock. Becca's skin was pulsing up and down as though there were *things* wriggling around just beneath the surface.

'What the hell is that?' Chris asked.

Victoria pulled Becca's top back down, covering her stomach once again. 'I don't know. I've never seen anything like this before.'

John panicked. 'We can't just leave her like this. We need to do something. We need to get her out of here!' He knew his words were fruitless. He'd heard what the commander had only just said about them being trapped there until they were released, crushed or suffocated to death and no matter how desperate he was to help the poor girl, there was nothing they could do in getting her up to the surface and away to a hospital.

'The drugs aren't working. She's in a lot of pain... I mean, I don't know what I am dealing with here but...' Victoria hesitated a moment before she continued with her suggestion, 'I can take a look...'

'Cut her open?' Chris looked at her, concerned as Becca continued screaming through the pain.

'It might be something I can remove...'

'We don't know what it is!' Chris continued.

'No, we don't, but if we leave her like this then it *will* kill her. Honestly as loathed as I am to say it, I firmly believe this is her only chance.'

'Do it, for God's sake do it,' John said.

It was John's money funding everything but that didn't make him the one in charge. Victoria turned to the commander of the submarine and looked to him for the go ahead. There was a slight delay as he watched Becca squirm and scream. Without looking directly to Victoria, he nodded for the go ahead.

Chapter Three

BEFORE

Jennifer Brooks dragged her case through to one of the cabins. Yolanda Lamas was already in there with her own case on the lower bunk, open and in the process of being unpacked into one of the sets of drawers available. When she noticed Jennifer there, she glanced up and smiled warmly. The pair had been introduced, along with everyone else, the night before but - until now - didn't know they were going to be sharing a room.

'I wondered who I'd be sharing with,' Yolanda said.

Jennifer noticed Yolanda's bag on the lower bunk. 'I'm top?'

'If that's okay with you.'

Jennifer would have preferred the lower, if only for if she felt poorly during the night, but she wasn't about to start fighting over a bed, especially when Yolanda had got there first. She answered, 'Sure.'

'I'll just get my bag sorted and then you can put yours here while you unpack, if you want.' There wasn't much space in the cabin; certainly not enough for them to both unpack their belongings at the same time. Jennifer didn't mind waiting though. In fact, she preferred to wait as - now she was here - she wasn't sure whether she could go through with the expedition, even if it was the chance of a life-time.

'You'll be pleased to know I don't snore,' Yolanda said if only to break an uncomfortable silence.

Jennifer laughed. 'I'm not sure if I do. Hopefully not.'

Yolanda shrugged. She reached into her bag and pulled out a small packet of ear-plugs. 'This isn't the first time I've shared a room with someone,' she said. 'I've learned to pack accordingly.'

'Ah smart. I didn't think of that.'

Yolanda laughed. 'Neither did I on my first trip. I soon learned though…' She added, 'There's a fair few in the pack so if you find yourself in need, you're more than welcome to take a pair.'

'Thank you.' Both women started to relax in one another's company with each passing moment. A relief to them both that they weren't stuck sharing a room with a selfish asshole. Of course it didn't mean they would be best friends for the duration of the expedition but, at least it was a positive start.

The group had been shown to the cabin area first. They'd been told to drop their bags off and then meet back up with the Commodore. Chris had told them they'd have plenty of time to unpack their belongings later but, for now, he wanted to give them a tour of the submarine. John didn't need the tour but waited with Chris regardless just so he could hear the reactions of the group as they looked around "his baby".

Jennifer had felt pretty uncomfortable boarding the submarine so wasn't sure how she would cope with being stuck in it for a whole month. Her plan was to dump the bag as instructed, look around and get a feel for the place and then - as John's offer - spend the night and make a decision in the morning. Part of her knew she would get used to how cramped everything was and how warm the air felt down there but another part wasn't sure if she *wanted* to get used to it. As she watched Yolanda, and heard the enthusiasm in her voice, Jennifer couldn't help but wonder whether she was going to be the only one who'd pull out at this stage.

'Have you been on a submarine before?' Jennifer asked.

Yolanda continued to unpack as she answered, if only to get out of Jennifer's way, 'No. I can't say I have. It's pretty exciting though, isn't it?' Jennifer just smiled in response and, despite having just met her, Yolanda could tell it wasn't a genuine smile. 'You're not so sure?'

Jennifer pulled a face. 'I'm not sure how I am feeling at the moment to be honest. It's a little…'

'Claustrophobic?' Yolanda asked.

Jennifer nodded.

'I felt the same but, to be honest, we'll get used to it. Anyway it's only for thirty days or so and…' With more enthusiasm she continued, 'This is the chance of a life-time! This won't come around again.'

Yolanda was right. This *was* the chance of a life-time. If Jennifer passed this up, she knew she wouldn't get the chance again and never mind being part of a team which was getting so much press in both the "real" world and the "scientific" world… This was the chance to see something very few people would ever get to see for themselves. If she walked away from this, she would forever regret it. Maybe not today, maybe not tomorrow but the regret *would* come. Jennifer sucked in a deep lungful of air. She needed to do this.

Yolanda still sensed Jennifer's unease and reassured her, 'It will be fine.'

*

NOW

'I can't do this.' Tears streamed down Yolanda's face. Whilst she studied for her degree in marine biology, she had worked as an assistant to a vet. Back then, it had seemed like a good idea as not only did she like animals and want to help them but it also gave her insight into their biology too. Working as an assistant to a vet was one thing and this was entirely different. She said again, 'Please, I cannot do this…'

'You're the most qualified here,' Victoria said sternly. 'You think I want to do this? We do not have a choice. If we don't; she dies.'

'We're all dead anyway.'

'Not yet we aren't and we aren't just about to roll over and give up. Now pull yourself together and help me,' Victoria continued. The way she spoke made her sound as though none of this bothered Victoria but, in truth, she was shit scared. Whatever was happening to Becca was entirely new to her. She'd never even *read* about something like this happening. The only reason she was going to cut her open though - with Yolanda assisting - was because, if she didn't, she knew Becca would die from whatever was going on internally. Even now, with every minute arguing with Yolanda, Becca was edging closer and closer to death. Victoria calmed herself down. Talking sternly to someone on the verge of hysterics wasn't going to do either of them any good. She inhaled a couple of deep breaths and - in a calmer manner - said, 'We *need* to do this and we need to do it *now*.'

Yolanda tried to calm herself. She could feel all other eyes drilling right into her soul as they watched the two women arguing about the necessary procedure. Just as Victoria had to visibly calm herself, do too did Yolanda. She took in a couple of deep breaths. Slowly, she let them out before nodding. *She would help.*

Victoria let out an audible sigh of relief. She could - and would - have done the procedure without Yolanda if she had to but, she knew it would be better with someone there on hand, to help out if need be. She turned to the Commodore and said, 'We need her on one of the tables in the canteen. I can't do this in the cabin.'

Nate stepped forward and said, 'I'll help move her.'

'Thank you,' Chris said.

Victoria stood there a moment, collecting her thoughts, as the two men hurried off to move Becca from out of her cabin and through to the canteen area. After a few seconds she quietly spoke to Yolanda, 'Remember - whatever happens - if we don't do this, she will die. We don't have a choice.' Given the state of Becca, and the scope of what was needing to be done, Victoria was fully expecting to lose her on the "operating table". Under these circumstances, the chances of survival were slim. She knew that. Everyone did. There was still a *chance* of survival though and, no matter of slight that was, it was better than just standing by and watching Becca fade away. 'Okay?' she pressed.

Yolanda wiped her face clean from tears. 'Not really,' she said honestly.

Victoria smiled sympathetically. 'Makes two of us.' She nodded towards the direction the others went and said, 'Come on - the sooner we get this done, the better.' As soon as she finished speaking, she followed Chris and John. Yolanda hesitated for a split second and then followed along.

Chapter Four

BEFORE

With precision, the razor-sharp knife sliced the skin away from the flesh with ease. Carolanne Rosenberg smiled to herself before peeling the last of the skin away. Once it was completely separated from the body, she laid it out flat on a black tray just as she always did. A few minutes in the oven and it would crisp up nicely, just the way she liked it. With the skin off and ready to go into the oven, she turned her attention back to the rest of the chicken as John entered the galley, with his chosen team of scientists following close behind as he gave them the guided tour with Chris.

'And this is the galley,' John said with as much pride as he'd had for the rest of the rooms he'd shown off too. 'No expense spared. We've filled the cupboards with as much food as you could possibly want, catering for all tastes. We have all the gadgets and gizmos a chef could desire in order to help them prepare the best food and drink you've ever tasted.

Carolanne laughed. 'No pressure then.'

They had been introduced to the chef the previous night, at the same time as meeting the rest of the crew before they parted ways so the crew could come and board the sub. As John and Chris continued through the galley, Carolanne smiled at them and, in turn, they smiled back with a little nod of "hello".

'Probably the most important member of the team,' Chris said, half-jokingly and half-serious. 'So you might want to be really nice to her.'

'Oh stop,' Carolanne said, still with a grin. 'I haven't spat in anyone's food yet.'

'Yet?' Nate was quick to pick up on that.

Carolanne gave him an innocent flutter of her eye-lids and Nate couldn't help but to laugh. One by one, in single file, they left the room and Carolanne to her cooking. With the knife still brandished in her left hand, she turned back to the chicken. The carcass was one of three chickens she'd cooked up for their dinner later that day.

Carolanne set the knife down to the edge of the chicken's breast and slice the first strip of meat away which, as was the chef's right, she ate for herself. Perfectly moist, she thought. As she went to slice another piece off for herself, just to be sure it was definitely cooked properly of course,

Nate leaned back into the galley. He watched as she ate a second piece of meat.

'Caught you!' he said with an idiotic grin on his face. Carolanne had caught his eye the night before, when they were first introduced. Recently divorced from his wife, she was almost the spitting image of her in looks. The personality was vastly different from their first introductions: Carolanne had smiled sweetly at him and said it was a pleasure to meet him whereas his wife used to just tell him to "fuck off". Lonely and craving attention, he had a feeling he would be spending most of his free time with Carolanne who was, living in her own head, completely oblivious to Nate's immediate crush. The suddenness of his voice, piercing the gentle hum of the submarine, caused her to jump which only made him laugh. 'Sorry, didn't mean to startle you.'

'Aren't you supposed to be following the others?'

'I mean, probably? But I thought I would rather come and talk with you.' He was half-expecting her to say something to that but, instead, she just stood there with raised eyebrows, as though waiting for him to say whatever he had on his mind. Immediately Nate felt his face flush as his heartbeat quickened. If he was to impress this fine lady, he knew he had to say something and - what's more - he had to do so quickly. Or, as the silence between the two lingered, he could just stand there and look like a blithering idiot. Desperate to break the silence, he stupidly asked, 'So what's cooking?'

Carolanne wasn't stupid. When they met the previous night she thought he was friendly enough. It wasn't as though they stopped for very long to have a chat but now, with the way he was acting here, she could tell he liked her. She answered him, 'Steak.'

'Steak? Nice...' Nate shifted his weight on his feet as he looked around the kitchen, desperate for something to leap out at him which could be deemed as a "decent conversation piece". His eyes settled on the chicken. He immediately felt stupid. Of course that was what was cooking. He had even caught her eating some of it. His face burned once more and he tried to make a joke of it, 'So what cut of the cow is that?'

Instead of answering him, Carolanne just asked him, 'Do you always make small talk like this?'

Nate stood there for a moment, unsure what to say. After a slight pause he shrugged and admitted, 'I study earthquakes for a career… I don't really get to talk to women that often…'

Quick as a flash, and enjoying the tease, Carolanne asked him, 'You study earthquakes?'

'Yes.'

'So why are you at sea? Or is an earthquake the same as a sea-quake?' She raised an eyebrow.

Nate went to say something but stopped himself. He couldn't decide if she was mocking him or genuinely being serious. He shifted his weight from one foot to the other, once again, before he admitted, 'I should probably go and catch the rest up…' He waited for her to say something but, still, she just stood there watching him. When he realised she was done talking, he turned and left the galley. Carolanne laughed and went back to cutting the chicken up. She set the sharp edge of the knife against the flesh and sliced away another perfectly cut strip. Once cut away, the slither of chicken was set on a plate before Carolanne took the knife and pressed it against the meat once more.

*

NOW

Victoria slid the point of the scalpels blade across Becca's stomach. Becca wasn't unconscious as they had nothing to knock her out with, given they didn't think they would be doing such procedures. Instead she was being held down by Chris, John and two other of the crew. There was Billy Smith putting his weight down on her left leg and Nate on her right. Despite their best efforts at keeping her still, Becca continued to writhe around, desperate for the pain to stop. As a result Victoria was working even slower than usual, so as not to suddenly have Becca thrust herself against the blade of the scalpel, causing it to dig in further than necessary.

Yolanda watched on, ready to assist Victoria in any way she asked.

'Okay, here, take it...' Victoria handed Yolanda the bloodied blade. Yolanda put it on a small tray, on the side, close to hand in case it was needed again. Victoria looked down to Becca's stomach. Unlike before it was now perfectly still as though whatever was causing the movement earlier had simply gone away.

'What now?' Chris asked, curious to know what Victoria was thinking.

Victoria glanced up at Chris. She didn't need to tell him what she was going to do as it made no difference to the act itself and would only have him potentially question her. He would see what she was going to do when she came to actually do it. She took a few deep breaths in, just to steady her nerves. Then, before any more distractions, she pushed the tips of her gloved fingers down on Becca's stomach. She gently pushed down, like working on a boil which was ready for squeezing, and jumped back when a black eel-like creature whipped its back-end out of the cut slit. Becca screamed in agonising pain as those who were holding her down struggled to keep her in place.

'What the fuck was that?' John asked.

All of them were staring down to the gash. Whatever it was had disappeared back up inside of Becca just as quickly as it had revealed itself.

'Did you see that? What the fuck was it?' John asked again. Panic oozing from his voice.

Victoria couldn't answer him. No one could. Without a word, she pushed her fingers up inside of the gash, in the direction the creature had gone. She winced in pain as something bit her, and pulled her hand back in a flash only to scream when she saw that whatever bit her was still attached. With a crack of her arm, she whipped it off her bleeding fingers. The creature, snake-like, landed on the floor and immediately slithered towards a gap beneath the kitchen sides.

'Don't let it get away!' Chris demanded.

Jennifer jumped out of its way, unprepared and unwilling to try and stop it from getting away from them. Nate released his grip of Becca's leg and, with a quick step after the creature, he stamped his full weight down upon it.

No one said anything. They were all just standing there, staring at the squashed mess left behind from Nate's raised boot. Whatever it was, it was dead. With all eyes drawn to the crushed body, no one noticed Becca's stomach had started to ripple once more.

Chapter Five

BEFORE

Before, the DSV Limiting Factor, a single person submersible took approximately four hours to dive to the bottom of the Mariana Trench. Fifteen foot long and nine feet wide, the DSV had a titanium hull that was three and a half inches thick in order to withstand the immense pressures at the ocean floor. The submersible was built to dive for sixteen hours at a time but, allowing for things to go "wrong", it could stay submerged for a further ninety-six hours in an emergency. Ninety-six hours was a long time to sit and wait, knowing death was coming for you. After all, when you were resting on the lowest point of the planet it wasn't exactly an easy job to get you rescued. In truth, if you were stuck down there then you probably weren't coming back up despite the best efforts of those who waited upon the salty surface. That's ninety-six additional hours to simply sit there and listen to how your friends can't get to you. Ninety-six hours to slowly suffocate in what will forever be your tomb. It was a cheerful thought and one best avoided when undertaking such a journey yourself and try as she might, Jennifer just couldn't push the thought from her mind. What if they got stuck? What if something happened and they couldn't get back to the surface? John had explained they too had emergency oxygen supplies to use up, if needed. He also explained there was more than enough oxygen in his submarine to see them through the expedition but, Jennifer couldn't help think oxygen would be only one half of a solution if they got stuck. What about a spare engine if this one went wrong? What about another sub waiting on the surface to go and collect the passengers if this one broke? But then, how would that work? They couldn't exactly just open the hatch and swim across to the other submarine. They would be crushed within an instant due to the pressure. So many thoughts swimming in her anxious mind. Thoughts which, for some reason, were only really setting in now she was actually onboard the submarine.

'You look worried,' Yolanda said as she walked into their cabin and saw Jennifer sitting there. 'You okay?'

Jennifer nodded. 'I'm good. Was just lost in thought thinking about my family.'

'Ah. Say no more.' Yolanda was all too aware that thirty days was a long time to be away from those you loved. Especially when there were no guarantees they'd be able to communicate with them from the bottom of the ocean. One thing to be in space and bounce calls off various satellites but quite enough to call up from seven miles deep. Yolanda made herself comfortable on her own bed. She looked up to the frame which supported Jennifer's bed directly above her. Yolanda had used a piece of sticky tape to put a photograph of her own family there so they'd be the last thing she saw before she drifted away to sleep. As she stared at the photo, a smile on her face, she said to Jennifer, 'Well just a few more hours and we'll be taking the plunge.' There was a mix of emotion in her voice: She was both apprehensive and excited. She, and the others onboard, were going where most people would *never* get to go for themselves. By morning, when they set off, she would become a part of history. She smiled. *Not many people can say that.*

*

NOW

Yolanda screamed as the black snake-like creature wrapped itself tight around her neck. It had shot from Becca's open wound with a speed suggesting it had been fired from within; straight out and straight around Yolanda's neck. Victoria immediately grabbed at it and started to pull as it made repeated strikes against Yolanda's face, cutting her open with teeth like pin pricks. The more Victoria pulled, the tighter it throttled Yolanda until she were no longer able to scream. With oxygen running out, she dropped to her knees as John and Chris came to aid Victoria. Even with three of them pulling at the creature, their hands occasionally slipping off due to the slick nature of its smooth and slimy skin, they couldn't pull it away. Behind them, another creature of similar length slipped from a now-still Becca.

Nate reacted in an instant and stamped down on it the moment it dropped to the cold floor. Just as the earlier one had been easy to crush, so too was this one and its guts sprayed from its sides in a satisfying splatter. Nate turned back to Yolanda and the others in time to see her eyes roll to the back of her bleeding head. Her body slumped to the floor and only then did the creature release its grip. Quick as a flash, John crushed it with his heavy boot.

They didn't say anything. They just stood shocked. Only Jennifer, with her back up against the corner of the room, was making any noise as she openly wept from all that was happening. Unable to support herself anymore, she slid down the wall until she was sitting on the floor. Still no one said anything.

Chapter Six

BEFORE

The expedition team had gathered at the front of the submarine, where the viewing window was. It was a little after six in the morning and, as promised the previous night, they were about to dive beneath the choppy waters for the first time. They'd all been given the option to disembark and all had refused the invitation, even Jennifer although she still felt nervous about the trip. She just knew, if she backed out now, she would only live to regret her decision in years to come. She kept telling herself that it was only thirty days. In the great scheme of things, that really was nothing. Thirty days and so many impressive sights to see in this once in a lifetime opportunity.

'This is it!' Yolanda looked at Jennifer with a broad grin on her excited face. Jennifer smiled back even though her smile was entirely forced.

'And here we go!' John shouted with excitement as the submarine started to dive. Whilst this wasn't the first time he had gone under the waters in this submarine, it was the first time he was going to be heading to the ocean floor. He'd had the chance beforehand, back after they'd successfully completed all of the tests, but he had refused. He wanted to experience it for the first time, along with everyone else. Like an excited child, he snapped a photo of the viewing screen with his mobile phone. A quick upload to his social media account before the inevitable radio silence. The picture and the ones: *Here we go!*

The room they were sitting in was much like a cinema in its layout, but with far less seats. There was the super-strength viewing window, of course, and then comfortable seats for the scientists to recline on as they got the guided tour of what lurked beneath the surface. But with each of the seats, there was also a small screen attached to an arm; much like a passenger-television set onboard of an airplane. This television didn't switch to different channels from Sky television though, it just flicked through a number of display modes for outside of the submarine: Thermal vision, night vision and such. That way if things were too dark to see outside of the window itself, the guests could flick between the different modes to ensure they weren't missing anything. Really it was just a gimmick but with the aim being to run commercial trips down to the ocean floor in the future, it was stuff like this which would help sell such a voyage.

John asked, 'So what does everyone think we'll find down here?'

'So long as it isn't *Meg*, I don't care…' Becca said, still making reference to the entertainment industry; this time about a giant prehistoric Megalodon shark.

'I wouldn't stress,' Nate said, 'we could just torpedo it out of the way…'

'Not sure I want to kill it,' Becca said. 'I just don't want to get eaten by it either.'

'Well don't need to worry about that,' John said calmly. 'We don't have any torpedos onboard.'

Nate turned to John and asked, 'No torpedos? So what happens if we come across a Russian submarine and they fire upon us?'

John laughed. 'Pretty unlikely where we're going.'

'But even so… I thought all submarines could defend themselves.'

'You make it sound like we're heading into war,' John said.

'For all you know, we could be.'

'Given what previous expeditions have seen down here, it's highly unlikely,' John said with a smug grin on his face.

Nate turned away and looked back to the viewing window. Already, beyond the window, everything was murky out there. Whilst he agreed it was probably unlikely they'd be coming under attack by the Russians, he still would have felt more comfortable had they had torpedos onboard.

'I hope we find Nessie,' Yolanda said, referring to Scotland's infamous Loch Ness monster.

'Nessie?' Becca looked at her with confusion written all over her face. 'I think we're a good few thousand miles away from where we'd find Nessie. And we're in the ocean, not a Loch.'

Yolanda rolled her eyes and said, 'I bet you're fun at parties.'

'What's this button do?' Nate asked as he turned his attention back to the screen attached to his seat. Immediately a voice started speaking from the small, built-in speaker, 'Discovered in 1875, whilst exploring the oceans using sounding equipment on the HMS Challenger, the Mariana Trench is a 1,580-mile crescent shaped section in the crust of the earth. Found in the western Pacific

Ocean, it is the deepest part located in *any* ocean. It was named after the nearby Mariana Islands with the deepest part, the Challenger Deep, named after the two boats which first explored its depths: The HMS Challenger and the HMS Challenger II. The HMS Challenger II sounded the trench a full 76 years after the first Challenger did in 1875.

At least 36,070 feet deep, the Mariana Trench hasn't been well explored given the number of challenges involved with getting to that depth. To put things in perspective, if Mount Everest were taken and dumped into the Mariana Trench, then Everest's mountain peak would still be more than a mile underwater.

Despite the depth of the trench and the fact no sunlight can penetrate that deep, the water isn't as cold as one might believe. For the most part it ranges between 34 to 39 degrees Fahrenheit but there are also hydrothermal vents throughout the trench as well. The water which comes from those vents can reach 700 degrees Fahrenheit and its these jets of water which are responsible for sustaining life found down there, due to the minerals within, because *there is life down there.*

What makes the 180 million year old (approximate) trench more exciting is that, despite its hostile environment (lack of light and acidic conditions, as two examples), creatures can survive down in the Mariana Trench and - we probably haven't seen half of what is living there! With more than 200 known microorganisms and small creatures lurking in the blackness - scientists are sure they will find new species too, such as the new type of snailfish which was found on one of the expeditions…'

'Oh shut the fuck up,' Nate said as he killed the playback. John looked at him, fairly shocked with his reaction.

'Not a fan?'

'Just drones on a bit with the same tone… Just kill me.'

John laughed. 'Maybe I should have paid someone else to narrate instead of doing it myself?'

Nate blushed. He hadn't registered it was John's voice. Of course it was his voice! This submarine was his baby so it stood to reason he would be doing as much as he could on it. Nate tried to think of something to say which would bury him out of the hole he'd put himself in but - nothing came to mind.

*

NOW

Everyone, with the exception of Victoria, had gathered at the viewing area. John was standing closest to the "window" with his hand pressed up against the clear screen. His eyes were fixed forward to the only small crack of light out there. A little rip in the ocean floor, one of many they believed. The light was a burning bright orange which none of them could really explain, nor did they have the chance to fully investigate it before *it* struck the submarine and wrapped itself around it whilst refusing to let go.

No one was saying anything. They were all as equally lost in their own private thoughts as John was. Chris approached John and stood to his side.

'You can't blame yourself,' Chris said.

'I can't?'

'You weren't to know. None of us were.'

'But I could have prepared for it still.'

'How do you prepare for something like this?'

'Not something like this.' John explained, 'I could have been prepared for the need to defend ourselves.'

'And that would have meant more crew onboard. More crew, more money, less space for the team you put together and…'

John laughed. 'You say that like it is a problem. In this instance, I would rather lose all of the scientists and exchange them for a full submarine crew. Officers who could man the defences and blast whatever the fuck that thing is out there. A proper medical bay where we could do emergency operations instead of having to make up an area in a fucking canteen...'

'You can't blame yourself. You can't do this.'

'Yet I'm the one who chose not to have weapons onboard and I am the one who chose to bring us down here. My choices, my plan, my money.' John turned to Chris and asked, 'If not me, who is to blame?' John asked, 'Should we blame you? You should have seen it coming? You should have steered us to safety?'

'No one is to blame. It happened. It's not my fault. It's not your fault. It's not their fault,' he added referring to the others standing with them. 'It just happened.'

'And because it happened, all we can do now is stand here and wait to die.'

Chris had nothing to say. There were no words of comfort he could offer. The surface was aware of the situation but there was nothing they could do either; not immediately anyway. It would take time to formulate a plan and, even then, it wasn't as though they could just send a submarine down to collect the stranded crew. The only option they really had was to send a submersible down with some form of weapon device primed on it; a hope that it might dislodge the creature's grip but even that was a risk. For all they knew, they'd shoot at it and - in a panic - it would simply squeeze harder.

John turned around and faced the rest of the room. Some people were looking down to the floor, lost in thought. Others, tears in their eyes, were staring directly at him as though hoping he were suddenly going to offer them a way out of his nightmare. He couldn't even apologise to them. There were simply no words to be said.

'Excuse me,' John said as he made his way to the exit. Not for the first time, he just wanted to put some distance between him and everyone else. He couldn't stand them looking at him, with the guilt that he was already feeling. There was even a part of him which wished that thing that latched onto Yolanda - whatever it was - had gone for him instead. At least, for him, all of this would be over and he could just make himself comfortable in the Hell that was waiting.

John turned into the main corridor which ran through the centre of the submarine from front to back. He was surprised to see Victoria standing there; mostly because he could have sworn she was already in the room he'd come from. She was standing motionless, a shocked look on her face and staring directly into the canteen. John felt a wave of unease wash over him.

Chapter Seven

BEFORE

John was sitting in the canteen with the rest of the team he had put together, as the crew continued taking the sub down to the ocean floor. They were picking at a chicken salad Carolanne had put together for their lunch; a thought that, at this time of the day and with the dive in progress, they'd probably prefer something lighter lining their stomachs.

Before being welcomed onto the expedition, John and Chris had sifted through hundreds and thousands of applicants. So many people had stepped forward to be a part of this trip for various reasons and it was almost a full-time job in itself, figuring out the best candidates. Those who were short-listed were invited to a video-call where John was able to give them a further grilling but, now, it was their turn to grill him.

'Your wife didn't mind you spending all the money to make this happen?' Jennifer asked, cutting straight to the point.

'I don't have a wife.'

'Girlfriend?'

John laughed. 'No girlfriend either.' John had learned the hard way that, when you're a billionaire, a lot of women don't exactly say "yes" to going out with you for the right reasons. Instead of seeing a potential best friend, lover and partner, they just looked at him as a cash cow and would go on to bleed him dry. Five occasions now he had been hurt by women who'd gone on to accept all his gifts and trips whilst "secretly" been sucking on some other man's dick. It hurt and, as a result, John was much more guarded now, and not because of the money. He didn't give a shit about the money. It wasn't like he couldn't afford to treat these women to whatever they might have fancied. He had more money in the bank than he'd ever be able to spend. He just hated the lies and, ultimately, the betrayal when he'd discover they were fucking someone else. It seemed that, in seeing his money, most people forgot that - actually - he was just as much human as the next person and, yes, had feelings too.

Jennifer was almost jealous of him in that moment. Not because he had been hurt, she didn't know any of that. Just the fact he wasn't leaving a family behind to come on this expedition. Not even two hours into the voyage yet and she was already missing her family like crazy. She imagined it just being a nice "break" from reality for John. He could come out here, sit on the bottom of the ocean for the duration and simply switch off to the stresses happening up on the dry land. A perfect little vacation which would also happen to get his name in the history books. Not a bad deal at all.

'So how much did this cost? From start through to now? I mean we already know this isn't the first submarine that you developed with the other ones not going so well…' Nate asked, ignoring the fact it was both none of his business what it cost, and also fairly rude in asking.

John just smiled. 'You don't want to know.'

Nate laughed. 'Well I kind of do or else I wouldn't have asked.'

Becca leaned over and helped Nate out by telling him, 'I think that's his polite way of saying it is none of your business.'

'Ah. Okay.'

It was Becca's turned to ask a question. 'Okay so why the bottom of the ocean? I thought most rich people climb Everest. Then, of course, the super rich people like to take themselves to space or, at the very least, launch a sports car up into the orbit.'

'Simple.' John said, 'Because not many people have been down here. Did you know there are more dead bodies on Everest than people who have been down to where we're going? And how many people have been up to space exactly? How many of them to you remember other than Buzz and Lance? Sure, a trip up to the moon might make the papers but books don't get written about those who go up there anymore.'

'Ah so it is a vanity thing?' Becca teased.

'Sure. A bit. But also, I want to see what's down here. If I want to see anything of space, I can just go to YouTube and look at the videos people have taken up. I can look through pictures. And as for space? What really is up there to see other than a different perspective of our own planet? It's not like we're going to find life right on our doorstep, is it? Down here though... There's not many pictures. There's definite life...' With a buzz about him, John added, 'This is exciting... And, I want to see it all.'

*

NOW

'Victoria?' John called out to the medic who was still rooted to the spot. She didn't even acknowledge his presence. 'What is it?' John walked towards her until he was standing side by side with her and still she said nothing to him. She just stared forward. Instead of asking another question to be ignored, he followed her gaze into the canteen. His heart skipped a beat and mouth fell agape at the sight of Yolanda standing there with her back to them.

Yolanda's body was twitching like she was having difficulty into controlling her muscles. Slowly, with jerky movements, she turned to face Victoria and John. Only the whites of her eyes were visible from where they were still rolled back in her skull. Her pasty white skin had black veins showing just beneath the surface.

'I... thought she was dead?'

Victoria swallowed. 'She is.'

Both just stood there, unable to look away as Yolanda's mouth started chattering much the same way as a cat "chattering" to some nearby birds.

'What's going on?' Victoria asked.

John didn't have an answer for her and wasn't about to give any theories either. Quick as a flash, he leaned to the canteen's heavy door and pulled it shut tight. Whatever was going on with Yolanda, she could stay that side of the metal door and they'd stay this side. Once the door clanged shut, he screamed out in frustration and kicked his foot against it. 'This wasn't supposed to be like this. None of this was supposed to be like this,' he said as, finally, his previously swallowed emotions started flowing freely.

Victoria had no words of comfort to offer him. Even if they had, they would have been cut short as - from behind the heavy metal door - Yolanda started to bang her fists against it. Both Victoria and John slowly backed away from the door, not that they expected it so suddenly swing open but… Just in case…

John repeated himself again, 'It wasn't supposed to be like this…'

Chapter Eight

BEFORE

The submarine rested on the ocean's floor after diving down for a little over five hours. Their first moment in the Challenger Deep and everyone had gathered in the viewing room to get a glimpse of what lay beneath. They stood in silence, looking into the near-darkness; a sight that hardly anyone had seen before. It was eerie. More so because they knew there to be life out there and yet - they could see nothing other than these faint orange glows from the sea-bed.

'What is that?' John asked. With so many scientists onboard, he hoped that one of them might have the answer to his question but, no one said anything. Despite the brightness of the orange crack, it didn't seem to be distributing light above it as one might have expected. Instead, above the cracks themselves, the waters seemed almost blacker in colour.

'Ready to turn the lights on?' Chris asked.

'Can we?' Becca asked. Whilst she was happy to see the trench like this, in its natural light, she was desperate to light it up to see if they could see anything else down there. Perhaps, she hoped, weird looking fish swimming away from the sudden burst of unexpected light.

It was John's expedition. He gave the nod to Chris who radioed through to Billy in the control room. A second later and, beyond the viewing window, the bottom of the trench was illuminated with a strong, bright light. Still, just above the orange cracks, there was a blackness there which they now saw as liquid.

John asked again, 'What is that?' Still no answers given.

Whilst Becca was disappointed by the lack of life in their immediate proximity, with nothing even showing on the highly sensitive radars, she couldn't help but feel a little thrill of excitement towards the black liquid coming from the hole. 'We can get a sample of that, right?'

John nodded. 'Yes. Yes we can.'

Nate asked, 'Are we going to move from this spot at all? Like patrol up and down the trench, or something?'

Chris shook his head and said, 'No. We're going to play possum. You want to see what's down here, the best thing we can do is play dead. We move around too much and we'll just scare anything away. Don't forget we're a lot bigger than whatever's down here and most things will try and hide from us incase we're predators.'

The disappointment was obvious on Nate's face but he understood the reasonings behind it. Even if he didn't, it wasn't his trip to command. He turned his attention back to the screen attached to his seat and started flicking through the various viewing options. He settled on thermal. Weirdly, the orange glow out there wasn't showing itself as a much of a heat source at all. Given the look of it, Nate had expected it to be red hot with the black liquid of a similar temperature.

Chris asked John, 'You want us to grab a sample?' It was a rhetorical question; he knew that was exactly what was wanted but, even so, he waited for the command given this was all running on John's dime and knowing how much he liked to "be in charge". John nodded enthusiastically. 'I'll get it sorted.' Chris left the viewing area and headed back to the control room to give his crew further instructions.

'So how's everyone feeling?' John asked. He himself was buzzing with excitement. There might not have been much to see (yet) but that didn't detract anything away from him. He was still sitting on the lowest point on earth and, to him, that was something special. As he scanned the room, he could tell most looked suitably happy. Only Nate looked a little disappointed. He told him, 'Don't worry, I'm sure there'll be another earthquake soon enough.'

Nate smiled. That was why he had come down; to see the earthquakes and try and understand why they were coming more frequently now. Also, he wanted to see the impact these quakes were having on the trench itself. So as not to appear rude, Nate said, 'I'm just grateful to be here...' He added, 'Thank you for this.'

John's ego was swelling with each passing moment they sat down there. He laughed and said, 'You're welcome.'

*

NOW

'What the fuck have you got us involved in?' Nate shouted.

John and Victoria had hurried back to where everyone was still gathered to report on what was happening in the canteen. At first the others thought it nothing more than a sick joke to answer Nate's earlier question of what else could possibly go wrong. Only when they heard the banging themselves did they realise that Yolanda was "up" and moving around in there.

'Well if she is alive, why aren't you letting her out?' Jennifer asked.

'Because...' Victoria didn't even know how to say what was on her mind. Mainly because she realised how ridiculous it sounded. 'That's not her. Whatever that is, it is not her...'

'What do you mean?' Jennifer continued with panic very evident in her voice.

'I think one of those things that was inside of her is using her body as a host,' Victoria continued. Her statement was enough to hush everyone up, if only for a moment.

'What are you fucking talking about?' Nate asked.

'I'm not the marine biologist,' Victoria said, 'but even I've heard of The Feline Parasite as just one example of what I think could be happening.'

'The Feline Parasite? What the fuck...'

Before Nate could finish his sentence, Victoria continued, 'A tiny protozoan. Nothing more than a blob but once it makes its way to the brain, it can alter the behaviour of hosts like rats, cats....'

'People?'

'Yes, even humans apparently. Now we have no idea what that thing was which was inside Becca but for all we know it is acting in a similar fashion to The Feline Parasite. When it was inside of her, it was trying to make its way up to her brain to take control…'

'Then what?' Jennifer asked, terrified at the prospect of something being able to take control of another being. 'Then what happens?'

'I don't know!' Victoria admitted.

'And what does it want?'

'Given how it attacked the moment we revealed it, I'm guessing it doesn't want to make friends,' John said solemnly. 'We need to keep her in that room…'

'I feel sick,' Jennifer said. She wasn't the only one. With the stress of all that was happening, none of those left standing were feeling particularly wonderful right about now.

Nate turned his attention back to John and asked again, 'What the fuck have you got us involved in?'

John said nothing. There was nothing he could say. He looked to the floor, too embarrassed and guilty to even keep Nate's eye contact.

Chris stepped in and told Nate, 'That's enough. It's not helping anyone.'

'Yeah? How do you know it's not helping me?' Nate asked.

'Back off,' Chris warned him. 'I won't tell you again.'

'Sorry but the moment shit hit the fan, you're no longer in charge of diddly-squat so how's about you shut the fuck up?'

'I can't do this,' Jennifer said as she raised her hands to her ears. She hurried away from the group and headed back towards her cabin, desperate for some peace and quiet, if only for a moment. She got a few steps away from the group before she stumbled and fell against the wall as the whole submarine shook. Everyone fell quiet as the rumbling continued for a few seconds before stopping just as abruptly as it had started.

John asked Nate, 'Another earthquake?'

Nate shook his head. The earthquakes caused vibrations throughout the vessel which varied in their strength depending on how bad the earthquake was. This was something else. *It* was shifting its weight against the submarine. No one spoke. They just stood there, holding the walls and wondering whether it was about to crush them.

A couple of minutes passed. Nate asked, 'At what point did you start regretting the decision not to have torpedos?'

John didn't give him the satisfaction of an answer.

Chapter Nine

BEFORE

'I could just look out there forever,' Becca said as she continued staring out of the viewing window. Her mind was picturing all the creatures out there, waiting to be discovered.

'One thing I don't understand,' Nate said to her, 'is how do things live down here? I mean look out there - there's no plant life for them to feed on.' He was right. The ocean floor was nothing but grains of sand as far as their artificial light could see. 'I mean I know they could eat each other but they found a sea-snail down here. Call me crazy but I can't see a sea-snail being much of an apex predator, you know?'

Becca said, 'They rely on decaying matter.'

'Decaying matter?'

'Sure. From dead creatures from the upper parts of the ocean. Bits sink. Bits get eaten. It's a little more complex than that, for sure, but it gives you an idea without having to go into too much detail.'

'That is insane.'

Becca added, 'And of course some of the things down here will most definitely eat the other things too. Can't rule that out.'

Nate was staring out of the viewing window to the nothingness before him. He shook his head and laughed. 'And we're supposed to believe there was a massive prehistoric shark living down here? I guess that author just relied on people not actually knowing that much about the trench, huh?'

'Hey, it was a fun book. I'm willing to suspend disbelief for giant sharks any day of the week,' Becca said.

'I guess I prefer my horror to have a little more reality to it,' Nate said.

Becca added, 'Not sure a horror book about a sea-snail found in the trench would really sell.'

Nate laughed. 'Depends on the author. I bet Stephen King could do it.'

'Here we go,' John said from the other side of the room, breaking up their conversation. He pointed to outside of the viewing window where a small, purpose-built miniature submersible had suddenly appeared in the light offered by the main sub. Operated by remote, this small submersible had been built specifically for collecting any samples of interest. It was, by all standards, unimpressive to look at but the technology behind it was as impressive as what powered the main submarine.

Becca watched with excitement as a small titanium arm stretched out towards the black liquid coming from the crack in the sea-bed. In its robotic grip, it had a beaker which had also been purposefully built to withstand the immense pressure. 'This is amazing,' Becca said. 'I never thought this would be possible.'

'Given the amount of failed attempts we had at getting this right,' John said, 'neither did I. Yet here we are…'

Along with pretty much everything else you could wish for on such a submarine, John had also installed a small laboratory. Whilst it might have lacked space, it certainly didn't lack in what it offered within though and - once the samples were back onboard - Becca would have pretty much all she needed to really investigate what they were dealing with.

'If it's a new substance, do I get to name it?' Becca asked, only half-joking.

John laughed. 'What would you call it?'

'Depends what it is. If it's toxic, I'd call it Steve.'

'Steve?'

'My ex.'

'Ah.'

Becca was like a little girl come Christmas morning, buzzing with excitement at the prospect of "discovering" something new. 'I wonder what it is,' she said.

'Well, you won't be wondering much longer...' John pointed beyond the window again. The little submersible was already making its way back to the submarine.

No longer content with just looking out of the window, Becca jumped up and hurried from the room. As she left she shouted, 'I've got to go see what it is.'

John smiled. With her enthusiasm clearly on show, he knew he had given the job to the right person. He'd give her a little "play-time" and then he'd go down and see what she'd discovered. 'All we need now is a massive earthquake and then you'll have happy too,' he said to Nate.

'Well not sure I'd wish another tsunami on the nearby islands but, a little earthquake might be nice,' Nate said.

*

NOW

John had had enough of Nate and how he kept on drilling in that it was all John's fault, like he wasn't already aware of that himself. As Nate asked again about the wish to go back in time and have torpedos installed, John changed the subject back to something closer to home for Nate. 'Didn't you say you wanted a little earthquake not so long ago? If memory serves correctly you said it would be nice… Well, here you go, I fucking delivered for you…'

Nate lunged for John with fists clenched but was pulled back by Chris before he could do anything, such as swing a punch. Chris knew the tension had been escalating towards physical violence. It was only a matter of time with the pressure mounting within the submarine. With strength, Chris shoved Nate back and blocked his path towards John if he were stupid enough to make another move for him.

'That's enough,' Chris said.

'Fuck you,' Nate spat. He looked past Chris to where John was standing. 'I wanted to know why the trench was having quakes more frequently. I didn't want to be tossed about like a fucking salt shaker by some… *Whatever the fuck it is out there!*'

'None of us wanted this,' Chris said.

'I'm sorry, I don't want to interrupt but what are we going to do about... *her*?' Jennifer spoke up from the corner. She was referring to Yolanda who was still banging up against the metal door separating her from the rest of the group. Jennifer's question calmed them down as they all - once again - became very aware of the banging.

Victoria looked at Chris who, from his face, clearly had no idea how best to handle this situation. She said, 'We can't open the door. Those creatures, whatever they were, made it very clear they're not friendly towards us. If we open that door, we do not know how it will react, or how strong it will be. We also don't know what else it is capable of.'

Chris sighed. He turned to John and said, 'Remember that fee you proposed? I'm going to need more. I am not being paid enough for this.'

John quietly said, 'If you get us out of this, I'll gladly pay you treble.'

All fell silent. The submarine's engine continued to quietly hum away as, from the canteen, Yolanda continued banging against the metal door.

Bang.

Bang.

Bang.

Bang.

Jennifer started to cry once more. 'Can we please just stop her from banging on the fucking door?'

Bang.

Bang.

Bang.

Chapter Ten

BEFORE

John woke with a start as - all around him - the bed shook violently and doors banged. In a daze from his disturbed dream and unsure what was going on, he grabbed the wall next to his bed in the hope of steadying himself but all that did was make him realise it wasn't just his bed shaking but the whole room. Fearful that the top bunk might collapse on him at any moment, John rolled from his bed and fell to the floor with a heavy thud. Books, on the narrow shelf along the opposite side of the fall, soon joined him down there as they tumbled from where they'd been balanced.

To save from anything landing on his head, John quickly crawled to the cabin's doorway and waited there until the vibrations stopped. By the time they had, he was fully awake with a racing heart and fully aware of what had just happened. His first ever earthquake. He smiled to himself, *Nate would be happy.* Except, Nate wasn't.

*

The quake had measured a six on the Richter scale which was pretty "average" for what had been happening down there over the last few months where they'd be mostly around that level, with a few going up to a nine.

Nate was standing at the viewing window. His own laptop was open on the seats close to where he had been working; inputting the figures and other bits of data. His eyes were fixed firmly to an orange crack in the sea-bed which had been about ten inches before but, was now more than three times the length.

The door opened behind him and John walked in with a grin on his face. 'There you go,' John said, 'one earthquake as promised.' To John, it was just a little "shake and go", he hadn't stopped to think about the possibilities of another tsunami, the loss of lives or anything else. 'What was it? Felt like a big one to me.' He added, 'Scared the shit out of me if I'm honest…' John noticed Nate's concerned look. 'All good?'

'That crack down there got bigger. Not just that one either but,' he pointed to the distance, 'the one further down there too.'

'That's bad?'

Nate shrugged. 'I mean, it isn't going to be good. The whole lay of the land down here is shifting down here and the quakes aren't showing any signs of slowing so... What will all this look like by the time it is finished? Will it finish? How many more tsunamis are we going to be subjected to? Also, if it is happening here, can it happen elsewhere too? Is this the start of something so much bigger?'

John hesitated a moment. He had no answer to all of the questions. He just shrugged and said, 'Well, that's why you're here, isn't it? To answer all those questions?'

Nate raised his eyebrows. Seeing it for himself now, he wasn't sure if he *could* answer the questions. Certainly not in the time they were down there for. Some people have studied this kind of thing their entire life and never come close to the answers they sought. For all he knew this was going to consume his life and he'd never know what was really happening.

John pointed to the orange substance. He asked, 'Is that magma?'

Nate nodded.

'How is that even possible? Surely it would just solidify the moment it broke through to the surface?'

Nate laughed. 'Science.' He had enough on his mind without stopping to give a science lesson to someone who clearly had no idea how these things worked and, most likely, probably didn't even care, either. Nate walked back over to his laptop. He picked it up and started filling in more boxes which were already on-screen. John waited a moment, unsure whether there was going to be a real answer coming at any point.

'Well,' John said, 'I guess I'll try and get a little more sleep then. Catch up with you in a few hours,' he added.

'Sure.'

As John turned away, the ground beneath him started to shake more violently than before. Both he and Nate tripped to the floor in a crumpled heap as, through the viewing window, the seabed opened and-

'What the fuck is that?!'

-a large tentacle, black in colour, pushed up through from beneath. Both men watched in awe and fascination - and fear - as it swayed there like a stray piece of sea-weed dancing in the current...

'Are you fucking seeing this?!'

Before an answer could come, the tentacle stopped dancing and stood fully erect for just a second before it pointed down to the submarine like an eel-like finger.

'Tell me you're fucking seeing this!'

The "finger" slowly snaked its way through the murky waters towards the vessel before it wrapped itself slowly around it; an anaconda snaring its prey.

'It's going to crush us! It's going to fucking kill us!'

*

NOW

Billy Smith and Chris stood by the canteen door. With no weapons onboard, both men were armed with whatever sharp implement they'd managed to pilfer from the sub's galley. The others were standing a little further away, down the corridor, with concerned looks on their faces. With a majority vote "for", the plan had been set to get into the canteen and kill the creature which had taken control of Yolanda's deceased body. Whilst some weren't up for doing this, most notably Jennifer who'd become quite attached to her cabin-mate, the argument had been that this wasn't Yolanda. They didn't know what it was but the simple fact was: Yolanda had been killed. Whatever was inside of her now, controlling her, had killed her. Whatever it was, this weird eel-like creature, it was hostile and dangerous. Those who voted "for" knew they couldn't just leave it locked away in a room. For now it was just banging against the door, trying to break through. How long before it figured out how to open it? Then what? Would it immediately try and kill the others? Could it infect them? Could it have their bodies taken over as well? Whatever it was, it needed to die and the sooner, the better.

'I can't watch this,' Jennifer said.

Jennifer about turned and started to walk away only to stop when Chris shouted, 'You need to stay here. Don't watch, fair enough, but we need to stay together. It's safer for all of us…'

Jennifer didn't turn back around. She just stayed with her back to the group and her eyes closed. Aware that noise would soon be a very real factor, she raised her hands up to her ears too to block it all out.

Chris turned to Billy and asked, 'Ready?'

Billy nodded. 'Let's do it.'

Chris gave John the nod. The plan was simple: John was to open the door, Chris and Billy were to rush in and terminate the creature on the other side. For this, the two men had chosen two of the biggest knives they'd found in the kitchen, not that Carolanne had stopped them. Funnily enough, since everything had gone so fucking wrong, cooking had been the last thing on her mind. If anyone wanted to eat, they could fend for themselves. The food was right there, in the galley, after all.

John hesitated a moment. He took in a few deep breaths, letting each one out slowly. Then, he nodded to himself and just as he went to pull the door open; everything fell silent from the other side.

Chapter Eleven

BEFORE

Chris hurried into the small room in which Becca was investigating the black matter they'd earlier brought in with the remote-controlled submarine. Before he had a chance to say anything she said, 'Think those quakes are done for the time being? I almost dropped this...' She was holding a beaker of black, swirling liquid in her hands. 'It would be nice if whatever was causing it gave us a little warning first, right?'

'Sorry but we need you to come to the observation room...' Chris couldn't hide the apprehensive look on his face.

'What is it?' she asked nervously.

'Well, we're kind of hoping you can tell...'

Before he could finish his sentence, the submarine juddered from side to side once again. This wasn't from a quake but - instead - it was from whatever *thing* had a grip of them. Such was the force of the shudder, the beaker slipped from Becca's hand. She screamed as the glass container shattered on the desk, spilling the contents in the process. 'Shit, shit, shit...' The moment the juddering stopped, she hurried over to the side cupboard and pulled out another beaker. 'Help me get it back...'

Chris interrupted her, 'I'm sorry but - really - you need to see this. This takes priority over everything else.'

Close to the table again, Becca stopped in her tracks and looked at Chris's concerned face. 'What is it?' But now Chris's attention had been stolen away. His eyes fixed firmly on the black liquid on the table which was "coming together" in a similar form to mercury. Becca followed his gaze and just stood there, open-mouthed. 'It wasn't acting like this earlier,' she said. 'Something's changed...' She leaned down closer to the table, to get a better look as the black mess formed itself into a jelly-like mass. 'I've never seen anything quite like this...'

'Are you sure you should be getting so close?'

An unknown substance, miles from any potential help, and Chris couldn't help but wonder as to whether she should be wearing hazard gear when getting so close to whatever the hell it was.

Chris jumped - startled - as the substance suddenly ejaculated itself over Becca's face. Immediately she fell back, screaming and clawing at her face, desperate to try and wipe it clean.

'Victoria!' Chris screamed as he hurried over to Becca's side without thinking as to whether the "ink" could do the same to his own face. By the time he got down on his knees, next to where Becca lay, her body was still. The liquid, for want of a better word, was pooled over her face. It was pulsing. Bubbling. Unsure what it was and what was happening to Becca with it sitting here, he didn't dare touch it. He yelled for the medic again, 'Victoria!' Unsure what to do, he sat there and quietly tried to reassure Becca, 'Everything's going to be okay…' With her body so still, he wasn't sure if she could hear him, or was registering anything that was happening but it didn't matter. If there was a chance she could hear him, he would keep saying it. 'Everything is going to be okay.'

*

NOW

'What's happening?' Yolanda was sitting on the galley floor with tears streaming from her eyes and running down her cheeks. Her complexion was pale and her hair hung in knots. She looked tired but, she looked like Yolanda at least. Despite her "normal" appearance, and the fact she was visibly upset, no one rushed forward to her assistance. Not even Jennifer, probably the person closest person to her given how they shared a cabin.

'Why have you got those?' Yolanda's eyes fixed to the blades which both Chris and Billy held in their hands. Both men looked down to their hands, almost as though they'd forgotten what they were clutching onto. Billy glanced from knife to Chris, waiting to see what he was going to do and ready to follow his lead. Chris was just standing there, unsure of everything.

'What's your name?' Victoria came forward. As medic, she had to take charge of the situation.

'What do you mean, what's my name?' Yolanda looked at her with a confused expression on her face.

'Just answer the question.'

'Yolanda.'

'Yolanda...?'

'Lamas.'

Victoria asked, 'And where are you?'

Yolanda continued to cry. 'I don't understand. What do you mean?'

'Right now, where are you?'

'I'm on the submarine. We're investigating what's happening in the Mariana Trench... Why is everyone looking at me like I've lost my fucking mind?'

Victoria glanced to Chris and shrugged. From how it looked, this was Yolanda but there was no way of knowing for sure if it really was. The questions being asked now were answered without much hesitation and gave the impression everything was okay but - what if whatever took her over had access to all that information too? Victoria couldn't recall anything like this had ever happened before so how could she tell whether her questions were a way of proving anything?

'Why is everyone looking at me like I've lost my mind?' Yolanda asked again.

Billy asked Chris, 'What do we do?'

Chris didn't know. The honest answer was, he had *no* idea what to do now.

'What is going on?' Yolanda asked.

After another lengthy pause, Chris finally gave an answer, 'Seal the door.'

As Billy started to close the door on her, Yolanda's expression suddenly changed. Her eyes turned black and she jumped to her feet with an inhuman screech from her throat which took all by surprise. Billy slammed the heavy metal door shut and spun the circular handle, sealing the door up tight in the process.

Immediately, Yolanda started banging on the door again.

'Whatever that is,' Chris said, 'that is not Yolanda anymore.'

Jennifer started to cry again. For the briefest of moments, she thought her friend was "okay". Now she knew for sure, she was never coming back. Whatever that was in the canteen, it was not Yolanda.

Yolanda was dead.

Chapter Twelve

BEFORE

Chris watched on as Victoria checked Becca's pulse by holding her wrist. He stayed silent as his brain tried to process everything that was going on. The old saying loud and clear in his tired head that, it never rained but poured.

Victoria gently lowered Becca's hand back down to the mattress they'd laid her on. Even her chest didn't look as though it were moving up and down anymore.

Chris asked, 'Is she dead?'

Victoria shook her head. 'She has a pulse but its weak.' She was quick to add, 'We need to get her to the surface.' Chris bit his lip. Victoria knew their predicament at the moment and how that wouldn't be a possible trip to make so there was little point in her actually saying as such. Victoria added, 'Not sure there is much I can do for her here. The liquid has congealed on her face and… It looks as though it is actually a part of her skin now. I don't know, it's hard to explain. Needless to say, I've not seen this before though and we don't have the means to even contemplate removing it down here.'

Once again, there was nothing Chris could say. At least nothing which would have provided a solution. None of this had been planned for (how could it be?) and none of this seemed to have an obvious solution. Eventually he said, 'Just, keep an eye on her okay?'

'Of course.'

'And let me know if anything changes.' Before he left the room, he said, 'I'll go and talk to the others.'

*

Chris had a pale look about his face as he turned to those who'd gathered. The faces of both crew and scientists looked at him with hope in their eyes. Solemnly he shook his head.

'Whatever it is, it has got us and it isn't in a hurry to let go. At this moment in time, we're trapped and unless it decides to just release us there's only two ways this is going to go.' They waited for him to explain further. He continued, 'One; it crushes the submarine. I don't need to explain what happens then. Two; it just holds us here until the oxygen supplies run out.' He stopped talking. A few people - already on the verge of tears - broke down and openly wept. Others just stood there with a shocked expression on their faces as they processed everything they'd heard, and all that had happened.

*

NOW

Nate, Billy, Chris, Carolanne, Victoria and John were sitting in the viewing area. Carolanne had brought all the spirit bottles up from the galley, along with some glasses. 'Enough for everyone,' she had said, ahead of pouring out the alcohol. 'No sense facing death sober.'

'I understand the lack of weapons. Fair enough. You couldn't have predicted this,' Nate said as he gazed out to the ever-growing orange crack on the sea-bed. 'But would it have killed you to put an emergency escape pod-type thing in here? You know, something we could have all jumped in ahead of blasting up to the surface?' He turned and stared directly at John, challenging him for an answer.

John down the remnants of his neat vodka, not that he was finding it easy to get drunk. All the alcohol was doing was giving him a bitch of a headache, unless that was Nate's constant talking. As John stared down to his empty cup, he said, 'At this point I welcome death.'

'What did you say?' Nate asked.

'Enough!' Chris shouted from the back of the room. 'I've had it with the constant fucking sniping. I don't want to spend whatever time I have left here listening to you fucking bitching. We're all in this same position and, you know what, hindsight *is* a wonderful thing but it changes nothing. It just gives everyone a fucking headache.'

'Oh shit, look everyone. Captain Cunt is talking. Everyone stop and listen. I'm sure there will be some sound words coming out of his mouth which will save us now…' Nate started sarcastically. He paused a moment, if only for dramatic effect. Then, 'Oh nope. Sorry. Just the usual absolute bullshit.' He shook his head and said to Chris directly, 'You are a fucking joke. No wonder you came on to take charge of this shit-show. No other cunt would employ you because they realised you're a joke.'

Chris got up from his seat and walked over to Nate.

Nate asked John, 'What's the matter? All your money go on putting this death-trap together and you couldn't afford a real…' Before he could finish his sentence, Chris laid him out flat with a single punch to the temple. No one was surprised or shocked. Nor did they run to Nate's aid.

Instead Jennifer said, 'What do you think she is doing now? I can't hear the banging anymore.'

True enough, down the corridor towards the canteen, everything was silent once more.

Chris spoke as though his sudden act of violence had never happened. He said, 'It doesn't matter. We locked the door. She can't get out. Just take the silence as a welcome relief and enjoy it while it lasts.'

John, staring out of the viewing window, said, 'The calm before the storm.' John had no idea how close he was to the truth.

Chapter Thirteen

THE SURFACE (NOW)

The surface had been rattled by the recent quakes once again. The seas were choppy and unforgiving to the boats floating upon the salty surface. With the submarine stuck on the sea-bed a few rescue boats had come out to the location with the crew trying to formulate a way of getting the stricken sub brought up. Whilst they didn't know the full extent of what was happening beneath the waves, they were aware that a creature had pinned the submarine to the sea-bed. Armed with that knowledge, one plan had been put forward which would see a number of remote-submersibles get sent down to where they were trapped. Each remote device being capable of delivering a short, sharp shock to whatever the creature was. A hope that - in shock - it might pull away from the submarine. Then, free, the sub would be able to make its way back up to the surface again. A very real worry, to go with the slim glimmer of hope, being that the shock could cause the creature to crush the submarine. If it squeezed hard enough and caused even the slightest bit of damage to the hull, the whole submarine would be instantly crushed and not by the creature but by the pressure down there. But if it worked... They could get back to the surface and have a story to tell their friends and family. Even if they couldn't move after being released, due to potential damage... The rescuers could at least hook the submarine and bring it to the surface that way. They just needed the creature to release its grip.

'Look we're kicking up a hell of a storm up here so we'll probably wait until things are calmer before sending the drones down,' Mike McGeorge said. He was on the radio, talking to Chris who had moved away from the group and headed back to the submarine's control room.

Not only were the waves getting rougher but, the skies had been hidden by a layer of thick, black clouds which were darker than the night-sky itself.

'I thought the weather was meant to be clear for the next few weeks at least,' Chris said. They'd only chosen to head to the Mariana Trench now because of the local weather reports and forecasts.

'Well that's just it,' Mike said, 'the weather reports are sunny skies and the usual heat. Clearly this came from no where but, hopefully it will go just as fast as it appeared.'

'I hope so.'

'Have you told the people what we're doing?'

'No. We have one shot at this and we don't know how it will play out. Don't want to cause unnecessary stress. Things are already fragile down here.'

'Well all being well, hopefully we'll startle this thing and it will fuck off back to where it came from.'

'Would be nice.'

'And you say it came out of a crack in the sea-bed.'

'Yep.'

'An octopus?'

'Never seen an octopus this big before now but could well be. Sure have been enough paintings of such a creature. Just never expected one to be living down here.' Chris said, 'We tried turning everything off that we could and going quiet but, still it wouldn't let go.'

'Well like I said, hopefully things will clear-up up here soon and we can get down there and shock the son of a bitch back home again. Until then, just hang tight, yeah?'

Chris couldn't help but laugh. It wasn't like he had any other choice but to hang tight. 'Can you do me a favour?'

'Sure.' A crack of lightening bolted from one of the clouds and stabbed into the sea-water with a series of bright blue-white forks.

'Can you tell my wife that...' The line went static. 'Hello?' Nothing. 'You there?' Still nothing. 'Fuck sa...' Before he could finish his sentence, the submarine and all around started to violently shake once again.

Up above, on the rough surface, Mike continued trying to get through, 'You hear me? Chris? Shit...' He set the radio mic down and looked up to the black skies. 'The hell is going on with this weather?' He was unaware that, the black skies weren't just over that stretch of the water; they stretched across all the seas all over the world and just as Mike and his crew were about to witness the storm of a life-time, so too was another crew about to go through its own hell.

*

Elsewhere (NOW)

Jamie screamed out for Hannah Sass as another large wave crashed into the side of the yacht. The force of which sent Hannah flying down towards the decking. With a crack loud enough to be heard over the high seas and rumbles in the sky, Hannah's temple smacked the very edge. When she didn't get up, Jamie made her way over to where she lay. The whole time she screamed for her to move as it wasn't safe to be on the deck but, Hannah heard nothing anymore. Her eyes open and fixed to the side of the boat. Blood seeping from the hefty crack in her skull.

Davey, the ship's bosun, came running out to help too as another heavy wave slammed the side of the yacht. With steadier sea-legs, Davey didn't fall. Without knowing what had happened to Hannah, other than that she fell and wasn't moving anymore, he scooped her up in his arms and carried her back into the yacht, out of the heavy rain which continued lashing down hard upon the soaked, slippery decking. Jamie followed with tears streaming down her face - not that you could tell she was crying given how wet she was. Unlike Davey, she'd seen that Hannah looked dead.

Inside, Davey put Hannah down on the carpeted floor and immediately started to check for a pulse. He pressed one side of her neck, then the other. He checked her wrist. He looked up to Jamie's face. 'She's dead,' he said.

Another crack of lightening lit the night-sky up.

Another rumble of thunder shook their insides.

'What the fuck was she doing out there?' Captain Lee was standing in the doorway, holding the door frame to keep his balance as the yacht continuing rolling on the ferocious waves.

'I don't know!' Jamie said truthfully.

'Is she…' Captain Lee cut his own question off when he saw the look on Davey's face. He punched the wall as a sudden burst of emotion surged through him. 'Fuck it!' As captain he was responsible for everyone on the yacht and in all his years, he'd never lost anyone. But then - in all his years - he had never seen a storm to this scale. He stepped into the room and slumped down on one of the many chairs. With ailing power and all comms down to try and get help, for the first time in his career, he felt entirely out of control and helpless. He put his head in his hands. The food was gone, bottled water almost gone… They still had the alcohol but it wasn't advisable to drink that given it only served to dehydrate you further. Although perhaps it would be worth it? Welcome death faster but do so pissed - at least that way it won't be as unpleasant. After a moment's contemplation, Lee told Davey, 'Round up the others.'

Davey hurried from the room, using the walls to keep himself as upright as possible as the ship continuing lurching. Captain Lee looked over to Hannah. Jamie was on her knees, next to the body and crying. He wanted to say "sorry" for what happened to her but the words were stuck in his throat. All he kept wondering was, *what was she doing outside?* For all he knew, she'd had enough and was going to jump overboard. She knew death was coming for her so figured she would do it on her terms. Captain Lee had heard of people doing that before; taking their own lives to go out on their own terms. "They" do say drowning is supposed to be one of the most peaceful ways to go. If that was what Hannah was trying to do then - congratulations - she got her wish, even if it was by different means. Given their current predicament, she was one of the lucky ones and - soon enough - it could well be they'd all be following her. The yacht was, after all, continually getting pushed by the storm. God only knew when they'd come across land and smash into it. For all Captain Lee knew, this could well be their last hour and soon they'd be drowning with the yacht capsized. In truth - they all had thought that at some point yet, weeks after getting stuck in this ungodly, never-ending storm - here they were… All still alive and kicking; just slowly starving.

Jamie said, 'You should have seen the storm coming. You should have been able to move us around it.' She was staring at Hannah but her words were aimed squarely to Captain Lee.

He looked back at her with contempt in his eyes. 'Is that right?'

'You're the captain! We have radars! You should have seen it coming!'

'I don't think you understand the gravity of the situation,' he said calmly. 'One minute everything was fine and then the whole screen changed. The storm came out of no where **like the gate's of hell itself opened up and swallowed us down…'**

Continues in the book "Below Deck"

Chapter Fourteen

NOW

Chris stumbled down the gangway, back towards the viewing room where everyone else was still gathered. From the canteen room, he could hear Yolanda laughing from the other side. As he passed, he hit the heavy door with the side of his clenched fist and shouted for her to, 'Shut the fuck up.'

'You're going to die down there,' Yolanda sung. The moment she finished her sentence, she started to laugh with glee.

Chris called back, 'As will you.' Under his breath he muttered, 'Dumb bitch.'

With the submarine still shaking, Chris stumbled into the viewing room. The others were seated, to save themselves from falling over, and watching through the viewing window as the black tentacle dragged them closer towards the gap in the sea-bed which had widened significantly.

John glanced over to Chris and said, 'I'm sorry.' From his tone, Chris knew that was all he had been saying to the others whilst Chris was up in the control room. 'I'm sorry,' he said again.

Chris looked over to what they were being dragged towards. Between the two edges of the sea-bed, staring straight back at them, he could see the beady-eye of the creature staring back at them. He didn't ask what it was. Not because he wasn't curious, he just knew no one would have the answers he wanted. He paused a moment. *No one would have the answers he wanted.* That wasn't quite true.

She had the answers.

Using the walls to steady himself, Chris hurried from the room and back down the narrow gangway towards the canteen door. Previously, after shutting Yolanda in, they'd jammed the door shut with a fire-axe from the nearby wall. He grabbed it from the handle and pulled it free. With the axe in hand, he struggled to open the door but - struggle as he did - he refused to drop the weapon, just in case "she" came at him.

Yolanda was just standing there. She faced the door as it opened. A wide, inhuman grin stretched across her face with such width that it would have hurt a normal person had they attempted it. Chris just stood there as the submarine continued to shake as it was pulled ever closer to the gaping hole.

'What is it? How can we get it to let go,' Chris asked. Whatever this thing was which had taken over Yolanda's body, it had clearly came from the same place as whatever had a hold of them. Maybe it knew what the creature was? Maybe it was able to communicate with it?

Yolanda laughed.

Chris raised the axe, ready to bring it down on her. 'We all die down here.'

Yolanda's laugh faded away. The smile slowly disappeared from her face which turned expressionless. Her eyes, black and soulless. She said, 'No. We all suffer down here.'

'What's that supposed to mean?'

Outside, unseen by Chris, the water around the split-hole started to get blacker in colour as the same toxic "liquid" from before started to pour out more freely. Whereas before it stayed "floating" close to the hole from where it came, now it started to seep out into the ocean itself.

Chris asked again, 'What do you mean we all suffer down here? That thing will crush us. There'll be no suffering, there'll just be a quick death.'

Yolanda said, 'Yes, followed by endless suffering as you relive whatever you are most guilty for - over and over - and the same fate awaits those who would venture down here to recover that which is lost forever.'

'You really need to start speaking English…'

'Or you need to start listening.'

Chris's arms started to grow tired from holding the axe up. Slowly he started to lower it. As he did so, Yolanda started to laugh once more.

She teased him, 'What is it which eats you up at night on those long nights in which you cannot sleep?'

'Fuck you.'

'What troubles you most and ties your stomach in knots?'

'I said, fuck you.'

'He will take your fears and use them against you for your eternal sleep. Your everlasting nightmare from which you cannot wake.'

'He. Who?'

Yolanda laughed again. 'He sees you. He has you. His poison has leaked into the waters and will infect and change those who are to stumble into it, bringing out the worst in man…'

*

ELSEWHERE (NOW)

As black water swirled around the super-yacht, Ben slammed the hammer down on the woman's head again and again. He wasn't laughing. He wasn't "happy". He wasn't angry. There was zero emotion. He was just getting the job done that the captain had asked of him. A job he had done time and time before, back on dry land before the new season had come into play.

Christina's body was lying on the plastic-covered floor of the galley which had been set up for this very occasion to save the blood staining into the yacht's woodwork. Her head was caved in. Blood seeped from her ear-holes, nostrils and even her mouth. One of her eyes was bulging from its socket and one more hit would have most likely made it pop all the way out.

Annette hadn't stopped to see the violence unfold. Neither could Davey bring herself to hang around to watch it either. The moment Ben first swung down - and connected - with the hammer, both of them made themselves scarce. Ben didn't mind. So long as they'd been there at the start, if things had gone wrong, in order to help if it was needed, that was fine. Other than that, once he got the hammering in and the body wasn't fighting back or struggling, he didn't give a shit what they did.

Ben dropped the hammer to the covered floor. He stood to his full height and looked down at the dead, pretty girl. It wasn't a waste. None of "this" would be a waste.

Before anyone else came in and laid claim to anything, he dropped to his knees and reached up under her black dress. He grabbed her knickers, sodden from urine after her life slipped away from her, and pulled them down. A quick little sniff and he pocketed them in his chef's jacket. A little souvenir for his memory box, to go with all the others he had taken before. The woman's purse, her jewellery, any potential gold teeth (not that they ever found any with people they'd done this too before) - Ben didn't give a shit about that crap. Stuff like that, he'd leave for the vultures to come pick at.

Ben grabbed a radio from the sideboard and spoke into it, 'Captain, Captain - Ben.'

'Come in, Ben,' Captain Lee's voice crackled through.

'It's done. Dinner is in the pantry.'

'Roger that, great work.'

Ben set the radio back from where he'd grabbed it. He looked back down to the body and wiped his brow free of sweat. 'Well,' he said with a little laugh, 'fair to say I've worked up an appetite.'

Continues in the book Below Deck

Chapter Fifteen

NOW

Chris demanded again, 'Who?' Little did he know that his question had already been answered in the viewing room, with the others still gathered at the window and the submarine teetering upon the jagged edge of the torn open sea-bed.

*

Nate stood, dumbstruck, as did the others who were now standing with him. All had risen from their seats as more of "beneath the gap" was revealed to them.

'How is that possible?'

The sea-bed had parted but there was not more water waiting for them below. The water defied the laws of physics and simply "stopped" at where the sea-bed once was. Beneath the water level, a wide open mass with red rocks and flutes of fire here and there, along with a darkness in the distance which looked as though it could have stretched forever.

All of them knew what this strange new land looked like but none were willing to say it. Wriggling through the air, as though dancing on invisible strings, more of the snake-like creatures which had slithered from Becca's open body earlier.

All of them jolted forward once again as the creature which gripped the submarine so tight, gave another tug of its outstretched tentacle, pulling the closer to the edge still.

*

Chris stumbled back and caught himself against the wall. Desperate for an answer, still in the galley, he asked again, 'Who are you talking about? Why can't you just fucking answer me?!'

'Some of man will be changed and some of man will be killed. Those who lose their lives will dwell in his own vice-like grip re-living their nightmares over and over. That is the way and what you and your friends look forward to now.'

Chris looked at Yolanda. What in the fuck was she? Whatever she was, Chris knew he wasn't going to get any answers from her anymore. Furthermore, he knew it wasn't Yolanda either. Whatever it was, it was hostile and potentially dangerous. Without a second thought - and in much haste - he raised the axe up high and brought the sharp edge straight down to the centre of her skull. She dropped to the floor with the axe still stuck in her head and her eyes - once again - rolled to the back of her skull.

'Fuck you.' Chris spat on her body as her leg started to twitch due to the nerve damage within the brain. With another shake of the submarine, Chris fell back against the wall. This time he made no attempt to steady himself and, instead, just slid on down to the floor. Whilst he didn't fully understand all that Yolanda had been saying, he knew enough of what was happening to know that this was it now.

His attention was stolen by more movement from Yolanda's body. Whereas her leg twitch had been subtle, her entire body started to violently convulse. Chris watched but made no attempt to get away. What would be, would be.

Yolanda's head turned to the side, still with the axe wedged firmly in her cranium, and her left eye plopped from the socket and - still attached - splatted on the floor where it stayed, staring back at Chris. He wasn't looking at the eye. He watched as the black eel-like creature slithered out from the ripped open socket. It landed on the floor, next to the eye, and curled itself into a tight little ball. Chris sighed. He knew it would only be a matter of time before it started to move towards him. The question was, would it be better to let it take over his body or would it be better to die with the outside pressure crushing him?

Neither option looked or sounded particularly pleasant.

*

John pulled himself up to one of the seats. He sat and, with elbows resting on knees, he put his head in his hands. The others were still looking out of the viewing window. They were crying. Billy was saying a prayer. Nate was just asking how any of this was possible over and over again as he looked to the giant mouth of the alien-looking octopus. Its mouth was open. Inside, along with razor sharp teeth pointed to spikes, there was a forked tongue. Closer and closer it pulled them towards its hungry mouth.

John didn't need to look out at the monster any longer. He didn't want to hear the prayers, the crying, the questions, the fear. He just wanted it to be all over. A wish that he could reverse time and cancel the whole fucking trip. A wish that he had listened to all those who'd said he was crazy for attempting such an expedition and how he was just wasting his money.

Quietly, talking to the group and yet unheard, he apologised again, 'I'm sorry for bringing you down here. I'm sorry for not being better equipped for all eventualities. I'm sorry for killing you…' This was his guilt to carry. The only relief came when, with a quick glance up and seeing nothing but the inside of the creature's mouth, he realised his guilt would be short-lived. Closer still they moved and - one final time - John said…

Chapter Sixteen

BEFORE, NOW, TOMORROW, FOREVER

John smiled to himself as he stood on the beach, looking out to the water. The smile slowly faded as a weird sensation washed over him, as though he had lived this moment before. Or, perhaps, a sense of dread that something terrible was going to happen.

'Beautiful isn't it?' Becca Ross said as she approached where John was standing. John visibly jumped at the sound of her voice. He'd been so lost in deep thought, he hadn't heard her approaching. As far as he was aware, he was the only one on the resort with most of the workers, trying to get the place fixed up, having already left for the night. Becca laughed. 'Sorry, I didn't meant to startle you.' She extended her hand and introduced herself, 'Becca Ross. I'm one of the…'

John took her hand in his and shook. 'I know who you are,' he said with a smile. 'I studied all the files ahead of coming out. I'm…'

'John Drain,' Becca said. 'And I studied all of the files too.' She asked, 'Are we the only ones here?'

'Other than the crew, so far.' He frowned. All of this was seeming too similar to him. Becca noticed the troubled look on his face.

She asked, 'Are you okay?'

'Just… I mean, yes. Deja Vu, that's all. All's good,' John said, half-attempting to reassure himself as opposed to anyone else. He turned back to the ocean and stared out in the hope Becca would changed the conversation.

Becca stood next to John and looked out into the ocean. 'It really is beautiful, isn't it?'

John just smiled. He could see why some would find the ocean beautiful but, to him, it was just haunting at night, mainly thanks to his imagination and the fear that, really, there could be anything lurking within those waters, unseen and waiting to strike. There was also the thought of how many people had lost their lives in the sea; not just this stretch of water but all around the world. As John looked out into the vast blackness, he couldn't help but to wonder how many lost souls were out there, in the darkness and unable to find their way back? The longer he stood there, the longer he was sure he could hear their cries with each lapping of the waves against the shore. *Imagine all those souls lost out there, or forced to re-live their mistakes over and over,* he thought. A shiver ran the length of his spine and he turned his back to the ocean, unable to look at it any longer. As he started to walk away, Becca quickly followed.

'I just wanted to say thank you for this,' she said.

'Not a problem. I'm glad you came.'

'Are you kidding? I feel like Dr. Alan Grant when he was invited to go and visit *Jurassic Park*.'

'Does that make me John Hammond?'

'You do share the same name.'

'Hopefully this expedition will go slightly better than Jurassic Park,' John continued. That creeping sense of dread still hanging heavy over him. Something felt off, he just couldn't put his finger upon it. *Hopefully,* he thought, *everything will be fine by morning. Probably just over-tired.*

The ending explained:

Look I get that you're smart cookies and don't need things spelled out to you. Unfortunately some people do and by the time they read my work, I've normally moved on to something else and my memory is shocking. So, for the sake of clarity... What if below the Mariana Trench lies Hell? What if upon discovering it, those who see it are killed? Those who die in Hell go on to live their most guilty moments of shame over and over. There is no escaping the pain they have caused themselves, or others. In this case; John blamed himself for putting everyone in this position so, for him, he would keep re-living those days over and over. But the real question is then, the one to really fuck with your head, is.... Was the start of the book the start of the story or had it already happened? With the **BEFORE** and **NOW** running at the same time throughout the book, what if they're running at the same time because they are *actually* happening at the same time?

With regards to why it flickered back to the book *BELOW DECK*, well that was just me having some fun really. In Below Deck we never know what happened during "the storm which came from no where". It was hinted at within the book, a worry from one of the characters which suggested the super-yacht could have gone to Hell. With that in mind, it made sense to explore that more within this book. The quakes caused the ground to open, Hell to reveal itself (if only for a few) and some of the evil to leak out. The demon creature in Yolanda (for I hope you realised they were demons as you neared the end of the book) said that some people would be turned (bad) and some would just be outwardly killed.

In fairness, just writing this down here, I realise this book could be a bit of a head-fuck to some people but, honestly, sometimes that is fun, right? Sometimes it's interesting to sit back and think about a story as opposed to just be taken on a gory little road trip. I mean, that is right, isn't it?

Hello?

Anyone?

HELLO?

Ah bugger....

Enjoyed the stories? Check out Vimeo for some of Matt Shaw's short films!

https://vimeo.com/themattshaw

Want more Matt Shaw?
Sign up for his Patreon Page!

www.patreon.com/themattshaw

Signed goodies?
Head for his store!www.mattshawpublications.co.uk

Made in the USA
Columbia, SC
07 July 2024

38237270R10069